Tadpole Books are published by Jump!, 5357 Penn Avenue South, Minneapolis, MN 55419, www.jumplibrary.com

Copyright ©2019 Jump. International copyright reserved in all countries. No part of this book may be reproduced in any form without written permission from the publisher.

Editor: Jenna Trnka **Designer:** Anna Peterson **Translator:** Annette Granat

Photo Credits: Eric Isselee/Shutterstock, cover, 1; Lynn_Bystrom/iStock, 2-3, 16tm; GlobalP/iStock, 4-5; Sylvain Cordier/Nature Picture Library, 6-7, 16br; stanley45/iStock, 8-9, 16bl; PhotosbyAndy/Shutterstock, 10-11, 16tl, 16bm; Betty Shelton/Shutterstock, 12-13; Coatesy/Shutterstock, 14-15, 16tr.

Library of Congress Cataloging-in-Publication Data
Names: Nilsen, Genevieve, author.
Title: Los cervatillos / por Genevieve Nilsen.
Other titles: Deer fawns. Spanish
Description: (Tadpole edition). | Minneapolis, MN : Jump!, Inc., (2018) | Series: Los bebés del bosque | Includes index.
Identifiers: LCCN 2018011208 (print) | LCCN 2018011873 (ebook) | ISBN 9781641280877 (ebook) | ISBN 9781641280860 (hardcover : alk. paper)
Subjects: LCSH: Fawns—Juvenile literature. | Deer—Juvenile literature. | Forest animals—Juvenile literature.
Classification: LCC QL737.U55 (ebook) | LCC QL737.U55 N55718 2018 (print) | DDC 599.6513/92—dc23
LC record available at https://lccn.loc.gov/2018011208

LOS BEBÉS DEL BOSQUE

LOS CERVATILLOS

por Genevieve Nilsen

TABLA DE CONTENIDO

Los cervatillos 2

Repaso de palabras 16

Índice 16

LOS CERVATILLOS

Veo un cervatillo.

cervatillo

Es un venado bebé.

El cervatillo aprende.

Camina.

Se esconde.

Come.

Bebe.

Crece.

Pierde sus manchas.

REPASO DE PALABRAS

camina

cervatillo

come

crece

manchas

se esconde

ÍNDICE

bebe 13
camina 7
cervatillo 2, 6
come 11

crece 14
manchas 5, 15
pierde 15
se esconde 9